2003 First U.S. edition
Text copyright © 2003 by Emily Horn
Illustrations copyright © 2003 by Paweł Pawlak

Published by Charlesbridge
85 Main Street
Watertown, MA 02472
(617) 926-0329
www.charlesbridge.com

© Siphano Picture Books 2002, for the text and illustrations

Library of Congress Cataloging-in-Publication Data
Horn, Emily.
    Excuse me—are you a witch? / Emily Horn ;
illustrated by Paweł Pawlak.
    p. cm.
Summary: A lonely black cat named Herbert searches
for some witches to keep him company.
    ISBN 1-58089-093-8 (reinforced for library use)
    [1. Cats—Fiction. 2. Witches—Fiction.] I. Pawlak,
Paweł, ill. II. Title.
    PZ7.H78148 Ex 2003
    [E]—dc21   2002013916

Color separation by Vivliosynergatiki, Athens, Greece
Printed in EU
(hc) 10 9 8 7 6 5 4 3 2 1

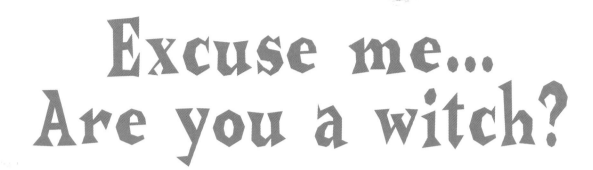

Excuse me...
Are you a witch?

written by Emily Horn
illustrated by Paweł Pawlak

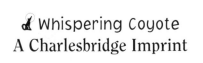

🐾 Whispering Coyote
A Charlesbridge Imprint

HERBERT was a cat. He lived on the street and didn't have any friends, so he was rather lonely.

On cold days Herbert went to the public library. It was warm and comfortable, and there were lots of good books to read.

One day Herbert found a book called
The Encyclopedia of Witches. It was very
interesting! Among other things, it said:

> *Witches wear striped stockings and pointed hats.*
> *Witches travel on brooms.*
> *Witches have cauldrons for heating up magic potions.*
> *Witches keep all kinds of pets—ravens, lizards, owls,*
> *and bats—but they love black cats most of all.*

"I am a black cat," thought Herbert. "If I find
myself a witch, perhaps I won't be cold and lonely
anymore!" So...

...off he went to find one.

As he walked down the street, Herbert saw a girl wearing striped stockings, just like the witch in the book.

"Excuse me," asked Herbert, "are you a witch?"

When the girl turned and saw Herbert, she jumped.

"Aaahhh! A black cat!" she cried, "That means bad luck!" And she ran away, as if she had seen a ghost.

"Am I really so frightening?" wondered Herbert. He sighed...

...and walked on.

Herbert heard a swishing sound.
He saw someone sweeping
the cobbles with a broom
just like the one in the book.
This *must* be a witch!

"Excuse me, are you a witch?"
asked Herbert.

The person turned around. It was a street-sweeper!

"Do I look like a witch?" he asked, laughing through his thick moustache.

"Oops," said Herbert...

...and went on down the street.

Then Herbert saw a woman cooking in
a big black cauldron, just like the one in the
book. She *must* be a witch!

Herbert walked up to the window.
"Excuse me, are you a witch?" he asked.

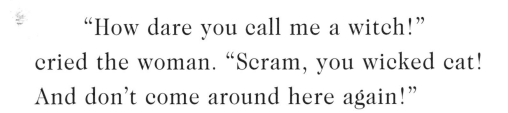

"How dare you call me a witch!" cried the woman. "Scram, you wicked cat! And don't come around here again!"

"I didn't mean to be rude..." Herbert said as he scooted away.

"I'm not having much luck finding a witch," Herbert thought, as he made his way back to the library.

He took a book off the shelf and started to read. He didn't notice the six strange figures behind the shelves...

...but the girls all noticed Herbert! They ran
to pick him up and stroke and pat him.

"What a dear little black cat!" they all cried.
Herbert was most embarrassed!

Just then he heard a woman's voice. "Quiet now,
my little witches! Remember, this is a library!"

"Excuse me," asked Herbert, "are you witches?"

"Of course," said the woman. "These are witch-schoolgirls, and I'm the witch-teacher."

And indeed they were—with brooms and striped stockings and pointy hats, just like the pictures in the book! And each one asked if she could take the little black cat home.

"My name is Herbert," he said, "but you can't *all* take me home."

"That's true," agreed the teacher, "but we *can* take you back to school, if you like."

"Yes, please!" said Herbert.

The girls all cheered.

Herbert beamed. Now he would have plenty of friends and never be lonely.

"Come now, girls," said the teacher. "Let's check out our books and go back to school. Herbert, you come, too."

"You're going to love being a witch-school cat!"